MR. MEN

go Cycling

Roger Hargreaves

WITH[

y name is
Can you
this book?

Origi... ... by
Roger Hargreaves

Written and illustrated by
Adam Hargreaves

EGMONT

Every year all the Mr Men and Little Miss take part in a bicycle race called the Grand Tour.

It is a very long race through many different countries.

Everyone practises very hard on their bikes before the race.

Mr Tall has a unicycle with only one wheel! To ride it you need to have very good balance.

And long legs.

Mr Jelly has a bike with two wheels.

You also need good balance to ride it.

Although Mr Jelly is a rather wobbly rider.

But not because he has just learnt to ride his bike.

Mr Jelly is always wobbly!

Mr Small has a tricycle with three wheels.

Which is easier to ride when you are little.

Mr Bump has a far more unusual bike.

It is an octocycle which has eight wheels and needs no balance at all.

Mr Bump had started with a tricycle and then kept adding wheels until he stopped falling over.

Mr Busy was very busy cycling everywhere.

He never missed a chance to practise.

He even cycled to the bathroom to clean his teeth in the morning.

And Mr Silly practised wearing flippers.

How silly.

I cannot imagine how he thought he was ever going to win a cycling race wearing flippers!

The person that everyone could imagine winning the race was Mr Rush.

This was probably because he had won the Grand Tour every year.

He was so fast that you could barely see him.

He was just a purple blur.

This year the race started in Happyland.

Little Miss Stubborn did not get off to a good start.

She stubbornly refused to go round the potholes.

And got a flat tyre.

Luckily, Mr Strong was on hand to blow her tyre back up.

Or maybe it was not so lucky.

Just one of Mr Strong's breaths was far too much!

After riding through Happyland, the cyclists got to Coldland where the heavy snow made it very hard going.

And poor Mr Nosey caught a cold.

It was warmer in Sleepyland, but now all the riders kept falling asleep.

Which gave Mr Lazy an advantage.

He could ride a bicycle and sleep at the same time!

The weather in Badland was bad.

Really bad.

In fact, it was atrocious.

But Mr Brave braved it bravely.

And then they came to the most difficult stage of the Tour.

Upland.

Where the roads only go uphill!

But everything that goes up must come down and the next day they rode into Downland.

Where the roads only go downhill.

Easy peasy!

Now, each year the race ends in a different country, but nobody knows which one it will be.

It was a surprise.

And this year the surprise was Nonsenseland.

But that was not the only surprise.

When they reached Nonsenseland all the riders had to wear flippers.

What nonsense.

How silly!

However, there was one rider who thought this was perfectly sensible.

And I think that you know who that was.

That's right!

Mr Silly.

He tore past all the other riders.

He even overtook Mr Rush.

And he won the race!

A win that no one could have ever imagined.

But then, as they say …

… practice makes perfect!